THE BRIDGE

THE BRIDGE

by EMILY CHENEY NEVILLE

illustrated by RONALD HIMLER

HARPER & ROW, PUBLISHERS

Library of Congress Cataloging-in-Publication Data
Neville, Emily Cheney.
   The bridge / by Emily Cheney Neville : illustrated by Ronald Himler.
— 1st ed.
       p.   cm.
   Summary: When the old wooden bridge breaks, a young boy is
delighted to be able to watch, from his front yard, the many
different machines at work building the new bridge across the brook.
   ISBN 0-06-024385-6 : $
   ISBN 0-06-024386-4 (lib. bdg.) : $
   [1. Bridges—Fiction.   2. Construction equipment—Fiction.
3. Machinery—Fiction.]   I. Himler, Ronald, ill.   II. Title.
PZ7.N462Br   1988   87-24941
[E]—dc19   CIP
                                                                AC

10 9 8 7 6 5 4 3 2 1
First Edition

For Sam
and his friends
in Keene Valley
E.C.N.

To Christopher Lindsay
R.H.

In the gray house on the hill lived Ben and his mother and father, and Chowder the dog, and Rhubarb the rabbit. A driveway ran down the hill to a small brook. The bridge was there.

Most mornings Ben and his mother drove over the bridge to go to town. Often they found a bulldozer to watch. Or a backhoe. Or maybe a dump truck.

Ben had learned the name of each big machine and how it worked. He was sure he could be the driver of any one. Afterward, Ben and his mother drove back over the little wooden bridge. It was made of planks laid on their edges, with cracks between so the rain could run through.

The car went over the bridge, and the planks went,
"Rattle-rattle-rattle! Here they come!"

"Here we come!" shouted Ben and his mother.

At the top of the hill, Chowder barked and turned round and round in circles. Rhubarb ran to her hole under the house.

Late in the afternoon, Ben played in his room. Soon he heard it.

"*Rattle-rattle-rattle! Here he comes!*" went the bridge. Ben ran from his room to the front door, and when it opened he threw his arms around his father's knees.

"What did you do today?" his father asked.

"Watched a backhoe digging. They're building a garage at the school. Daddy! Can we go ride on our mower?"

"Too late. Too cold. The grass has stopped growing."

Ben's mother said, "The oil man still didn't come. I knocked on the tank and it sounded empty."

"Is it broken?" Ben asked.

"Not broken, just empty. I bet Albert will come tomorrow," said Ben's father.

"In his big red tank truck," said Ben. "*Br-r-r-mm-Br-r-r-mm-Br-r-r-mm!*"

The next day, Ben was trying to balance the last block on top of his tower. He was holding his breath.

"*Rattle-rattle-rattle! Here he comes!*" went the bridge. Chowder barked fiercely.

Then the bridge went, "*Rattle-rattle-CR-ACK!*" But nobody heard what the bridge was saying.

Ben was running out the door, and Albert the oil man was listening to his boss on the crackly radio in his cab.

Ben watched Albert pull the hose, which looked like an enormous snake, out of the tank truck.

"What's your truck's name?" Ben asked.

"Haven't named her," said Albert, as he fitted the nozzle of the hose into the oil tank by Ben's garage. "What do you think?"

"Well, she's big and red and sort of round. Call her Hamburger."

"Some Hamburger! When she's full, she weighs fourteen tons."

The oil gauge stopped whirring, and Albert fed the snake back into the tanker and climbed into the cab.

"Don't forget to listen to our little bridge," said Ben.

"Okay," said Albert. He drove down the hill slowly and eased the front wheels onto the bridge.

"*R-a-t-t-l-e*," went the bridge.

Albert gently pressed on the gas pedal. Now the whole tanker was on the bridge.

"*CR-A-A-CK!*" went the bridge.

Albert slammed his foot on the gas. The motor roared. The cab jerked forward.

"*CR-A-A-A-SH!*" went the bridge.

Ben saw the tanker smash down into the brook on top of the bridge. The cab was pulled backwards, and its wheels reared up in the air.

"Mom!" yelled Ben. "The bridge broke!"

Ben and his mother ran down to the brook. They saw Albert climb out of the cab, down onto the boulders in the brook, and up onto their driveway.

Ben shouted: "How're you going to get the tanker out of the brook? How're you going to fix our bridge? How're you—"

"Hold it, hold it!" Albert said. "First I better use your telephone. My radio broke, and I've got to tell my boss to send a tow truck and an empty tanker."

Afterward, Ben and his mother walked down to the brook with Albert. Albert stared at the tanker, but Ben kept looking down the highway.

"Here they come!" he shouted when he saw the tow truck and the empty tanker.

Albert climbed down into the brook. He pulled the hose out of Hamburger and handed the nozzle up to the new driver, who fixed it into the empty tanker.

"Look! The road commissioner's coming, too!" yelled Ben. A bright yellow pickup truck came and parked beside the tanker. The commissioner got out but left his gumball light flashing. Every time it flashed, Ben blinked.

When the gauge stopped whirring, Albert pulled the hose back into the tanker in the brook. "Is Hamburger empty now?" Ben asked.

"Yup."

"Why?"

"So we can pull her out of the brook. With oil in her, she was too heavy, and the oil might have spilled. That'd be bad for the brook."

The tow truck backed up to the cab of Albert's tanker. The garage man fastened a big hook at the end of a chain onto the cab's axle.

The truck motor roared. Slowly, the cab wheels were pulled back onto the ground. Ben's toes stiffened as he pressed on a gas pedal. The cab moved forward, dragging the tanker out of the brook bed. Hamburger looked a little bent, but she still rolled. Ben let out his breath, and his toes relaxed.

The tow truck pulled Hamburger away, and the road commissioner followed in his pickup. Ben watched the flashing light disappear down the highway.

Ben and his mother looked at the broken bridge. There were no more machines to watch.

"I must call Daddy," his mother said.

"How's Daddy going to fix our bridge? How's he going to get home, even? Can he fix it Saturday?"

His mother didn't answer any of his questions. She just started walking up the hill.

"We won't be able to hear the bridge when Daddy comes," said Ben. He looked sad and followed his mother home.

After lunch, Ben looked at a book. He must have fallen asleep, because when he looked up, a dog was barking, and there was no dog in that book. Right away he remembered about the bridge.

Chowder was still barking and turning round in circles as Ben and his mother ran down the hill. Ben's father and his car were on the other side of the brook, by the broken bridge.

"I brought your rubber boots, so you won't get your good shoes wet," said Ben's mother. She threw them across, one at a time. He put them on and waded through the brook.

"Daddy, you missed it all!" said Ben. "There was the tow truck, and another tanker, and the road commissioner in his pickup with the gumball light. They all came to our bridge!"

"Great," said Ben's father, but he didn't seem to mean it.

"I could drive a tow truck, Daddy. I could pull that tanker out of the brook. *Br-m-m-m, Br-m-m-m!* Daddy, can you fix our bridge?"

"No, Ben, I'm not a bridge builder."

At the house, Ben's father made many phone calls, and he frowned a lot. But at dinner, he said, "They're coming at seven o'clock tomorrow morning. They're bringing a culvert."

"Who's coming?" said Ben.

"The men to fix the bridge."

"What's a culver-thing?"

"It's a huge metal pipe. It'll be so big I could walk right through it. They'll put it in the brook, and the water will run through it. Then they'll pile dirt on top for us to drive over."

Ben thought for a minute. "Daddy, are they going to dig?"

"They sure are."

"With a bulldozer and a backhoe and a bucket loader?"

"Probably all three."

"Hooray!" Ben ran around the dining table and sang, "A backhoe, a loader, and a bulldozer, too!"

Next morning, Ben and his father went down to the broken bridge just as the sun came up.

"When's the bulldozer coming?" said Ben.

"Soon." Then his father scratched a line in the gravel with the heel of his boot.

"What's that for?" said Ben.

"For you to stay behind, while I get ready to go to work. Now, where are you going to stay?"

"Behind this line," said Ben. After his father left, Ben jumped up and down, but he didn't let his toes cross the line, not even when the road commissioner drove up in his truck with the flashing light.

Ben's father came back with his suit on, his rubber boots on, and his shoes in his hand.

"Daddy, the backhoe didn't come."

"Keep watching. And stay behind that line." He waded across the brook, got in his car, and drove away.

Suddenly, down the highway Ben saw something big and yellow coming. Slowly it got bigger.

"The backhoe!" Ben yelled.

It stopped alongside the broken bridge. First it reached out with its long neck and picked up one side of the old bridge railings, then the other, then the rattly planks. Soon the broken bridge was a pile of lumber.

Ben looked back up the highway. There was another yellow spot coming. It was a flatbed truck, carrying a bulldozer and a loader with a wide bucket.

"Mommy! You've got to come see...."

"Here I am, Ben," said his mother, right beside him. "I brought you some breakfast."

"Wow!" said Ben. "A breakfast picnic and a backhoe and a bulldozer and a loader! All at our bridge!"

He squatted behind the line in the gravel and drank his juice and ate toast with bacon on it.

All morning long, Ben and his mother watched the machines work. The bulldozer caterpillared down into the brook, and its slanted blade pushed boulders and gravel and water.

"I didn't know you could bulldoze *water*!" said Ben.

The backhoe and the loader got in the brook too, and sloshed great bucketfuls of gravel and water up onto the road.

Ben looked up. Far down the highway something else was slowly coming. It glinted like silver.

"It's the culvert!" said Ben's mother.

The flatbed truck with the culvert stopped beside the pile of
wood that was the old bridge. The backhoe nudged the culvert
and rolled it gently onto the ground. A workman walked right
into it, took out his tape measure, and measured the height of
the culvert. He found a plank of the same length and stood it
up in the brook.

"Does the culvert have to fit?" said Ben. "Like a shoe?"

"I guess it does," said his mother. "I'm going home to get us some lunch. Don't go near the machines."

"Daddy made this line," Ben showed her. "I stay behind it. Why do I have to?"

"Well, if you got hurt, the ambulance couldn't come. There's no bridge yet."

Ben thought about that as his mother started home. "Mom! You be careful too. The fire engine couldn't come either."

It took a long time to make the brook fit the culvert. The brook bed wasn't deep enough. All afternoon the bulldozer pushed and the backhoe and loader scooped. One boulder buried in the bottom of the brook was as big as Chowder's doghouse. The bulldozer pushed and roared. Finally the boulder moved. Water gurgled under it. The bulldozer rolled it out of the way.

"What happened to my line?" Ben looked up and there was his father, right beside him. Ben's feet were in front of the line.

"Daddy, I'm being very careful. I had to watch them pushing that big boulder."

"Where's Mom?"

"She's up at the house. She's being very careful too, because the fire engine couldn't come. Right, Daddy?"

"Right," said his father. "I didn't think of that."

"*I* thought of that," said Ben. "When I get big, I might drive a fire engine. Or a bulldozer, and push boulders as big as a house."

The bulldozer crawled out of the brook and got behind the culvert. The backhoe's long arm cradled it. The bulldozer pushed and the backhoe held on. Slowly they eased it into the brook.

Ben and his father ran downstream and looked back into the culvert.

"Here comes the water!" Ben shouted. The brook started to run through the culvert.

The machines pushed and piled dirt over the culvert. Finally the loader chugged right across on top of it.

"Hooray! It's a bridge!"

"Run up to the house and get Mom," said Ben's father. "We'll all take our first ride across the bridge."

When Ben's mother came, they walked across the culvert and got in the car. As they drove across the new bridge, no one said a word. The tires made no noise in the soft dirt. They drove up the hill.

"Chowder didn't bark," said Ben.

"He must have been fast asleep," said his mother.

"He was never *that* asleep before," said Ben, and he saw that Rhubarb didn't run into her hole, either.

As he finished his dinner, Ben gave a great yawn.

"Hard work being a bridge superintendent," said his father.

When his mother had tucked him in bed, Ben said, "Mommy, our new bridge doesn't say *'Rattle-rattle-rattle! Here they come!'* Chowder doesn't know when to bark, and Rhubarb just sits there. I miss our old bridge."

"So do I, Ben."

"Mommy?"

"Yes, Ben."

"What can we do?"

"I'll try to think, Ben. You try, too. Maybe you'll dream of something."

Ben woke up with the sun on his face. He rubbed his eyes and said, "What we need is a bell."

He ran to the kitchen. "Mom! We need a bell for the bridge!"

His mother drank her coffee and didn't say anything.

Ben waited till she finished. "Can we start work now?"

"Doing what, Ben?"

"Fixing the bridge so it'll talk to us. I think we need a bell."

"Oh…a bell…" Ben's mother walked into the living room and rummaged through a drawer. "Here's this nice old cowbell I bought in a yard sale."

"What'll we do with it?"

They went into the garage, and his mother found an old, rusty spring and some wire and a broken metal lawn rake. She got a hammer and some nails and a drill, and they walked down the hill to the bridge.

"Help me get one of those big planks from the old bridge," said Ben's mother. They each carried one end. Ben's mother drilled a hole in one end of the plank, big enough to stick the rake handle into. She wired the old spring to one of the tines of the rake and wired the bell to the spring.

They buried the plank right across the middle of the new bridge. The rake and bell stood up at one edge.

"At five o'clock we'll come and wait for Daddy," said Ben's mother. "We'll surprise him."

They were out by the highway when Ben's father came home from work. All three of them got in the front seat. There was a little bump when the car's wheels went over the plank, and *"Ringle-dingle-dingle! Here they come!"* went the bridge.

"Here we come!" shouted Ben. Chowder barked and turned round and round in circles, and Rhubarb ran under the house, and Ben knew they were truly home, over their new bridge.